GIMME SHELTER

Misadventures and Misinformation

Also by Doreen Cronin

Cyclone

Bloom

Bounce

M.O.M. (Mom Operating Manual)

Stretch

Wiggle

The Chicken Squad #1: *The First Misadventure*

The Chicken Squad #2: *The Case of the Weird Blue Chicken*

The Chicken Squad #3: *Into the Wild*

The Chicken Squad #4: *Dark Shadows*

Click, Clack, Boo!

Click, Clack, Ho! Ho! Ho!

Click, Clack, Moo: Cows That Type

Click, Clack, Peep!

Click, Clack, Quackity-Quack

Click, Clack, Splish, Splash

Click, Clack, Surprise!

Dooby Dooby Moo

Duck for President

Giggle, Giggle, Quack

Thump, Quack, Moo

GIMME SHELTER

Misadventures and Misinformation

Doreen Cronin

Illustrated by Stephen Gilpin

Cover by Kevin Cornell

A Caitlyn Dlouhy Book

Atheneum Books for Young Readers

atheneum New York London Toronto Sydney New Delhi

atheneum

ATHENEUM BOOKS FOR YOUNG READERS
An imprint of Simon & Schuster Children's Publishing Division
1230 Avenue of the Americas, New York, New York 10020

For information about special discounts for bulk purchases, please contact Simon & Schuster Special Sales at 1-866-506-1949 or business@simonandschuster.com.
The Simon & Schuster Speakers Bureau can bring authors to your live event. For more information or to book an event, contact the Simon & Schuster Speakers Bureau at 1-866-248-3049 or visit our website at www.simonspeakers.com.
Book design by Sonia Chaghatzbanian
The text for this book was set in Garth Graphic.
The illustrations for this book were rendered digitally.
Manufactured in the United States of America
1117 FFG
First Edition
10 9 8 7 6 5 4 3 2 1
Library of Congress Cataloging-in-Publication Data Names: Cronin, Doreen, author. | Gilpin, Stephen, illustrator.
Title: Gimme shelter : misadventures and misinformation / Doreen Cronin ; illustrated by Stephen Gilpin.
Description: First edition. | New York : Atheneum, 2017. | Series: The Chicken Squad ; 5 | "A Caitlyn Dlouhy Book." | Summary: The Chicken Squad uncovers mysterious remains while digging a meteor/storm shelter, and they stop work to investigate just as a big storm is approaching.
Identifiers: LCCN 2017008516 | ISBN 9781534405714 (hardback) | ISBN 9781534405738 (eBook)
Subjects: | CYAC: Chickens—Fiction. | Holes—Fiction. | Humorous stories.
| BISAC: JUVENILE FICTION / Humorous Stories. | JUVENILE FICTION / Animals / Farm Animals. | JUVENILE FICTION / Imagination & Play.
Classification: LCC PZ7.C88135 Gim 2017 | DDC [E]—dc23
LC record available at https://lccn.loc.gov/2017008516

For Grace, with love
—D. C.

For Owen, and the mysterious things he
brings into the house
—S. G.

GIMME SHELTER

Misadventures
and Misinformation

Introductions

Neighbors.

Search-and-rescue dogs make great neighbors. We mind our own business, we're dependable, and we come in handy if you ever get lost in the woods. Chickens, on the other hand, are highly questionable. They get up too early, they squawk all day, and they have entirely too much time on their hands, which is never good—for anybody. These four are no exception:

Dirt: Short, yellow, fuzzy

Real Name: Peep

Specialty: Foreign languages, math, colors, computer codes

Sugar: Short, yellow, fuzzy

Real Name: Little Boo

Specialty: Breaking and entering, interrupting

Poppy: Short, yellow, fuzzy

Real Name: Poppy

Specialty: Sugarology
(will explain later)

Sweetie: Short, yellow, fuzzy

Real Name: Sweet Coconut Louise

Specialty: None that I can see

"Where did you get all that stuff?" I asked, annoyed at the crowd in and around my water bowl.

"Over there," said Sugar, pointing her wing in no particular direction.

"Over where, *exactly*?" I asked.

"Garage sale," answered Sugar.

"Garbage," answered Sweetie.

"Squirrels," answered Poppy.

"No comment," answered Dirt, avoiding eye contact.

Like I said, way too much time on their hands.

My name is John Joseph Tully—J. J. for short. I was a search-and-rescue dog for seven years, but my days of dangerous missions and daring rescues are behind me. If you like to play with chickens, they're all yours. And if a couple of kids come by looking for their stuff, point them toward Sugar and tell them the chickens come free with the clothes.

Chapter 1

"A little help here!" Sugar yelled impatiently from the bottom of a hole in the yard. The hole was twice as tall as she was and three times as wide. "Hellooooooo!!" She leaned on her shovel and waited. A squirrel leaned in and dropped an acorn on her head. Sugar threw it back.

"Ouch!" Dirt's face appeared at the top of the hole. "What are you doing down there, Sugar? And why are you throwing acorns at me?"

"What does it look like I'm doing?" Sugar answered.

"It looks like you threw an acorn at me and fell into a hole," Dirt replied, leaning in closer.

"For your information, I didn't fall into this hole. I dug it myself."

"Wait a minute. . . . Is that one of Barbara's spoons??" asked Dirt, leaning in closer still.

"Look for yourself," Sugar replied, holding the spoon close enough for

Dirt to touch—and then nudging her right into the ladle.

"HEY!" said Dirt as Sugar tipped her out at the bottom of the hole. "What did you do that for?"

"I couldn't get out of the hole on my own, and I am one hundred percent confident that *you* will get us out of here."

"That would have been a lot easier to do from up there!" said Dirt, brushing herself off. "Now we have to wait for Poppy or Sweetie to get us out."

"I'm not going to lie," said Sugar, "my confidence just dropped to about thirty-seven percent."

"I have an idea . . . ," said Dirt.

"Are you thinking that you climb into the spoon and I launch you out of here so you can find a rope long enough to pull me out of the hole?"

"No," said Dirt. "I'm thinking if we lean the spoon at just the right angle, we might be able climb up the handle—"

"HEY! Poppy!! I found them!" called Sweetie. "They're digging a hole for a pool! And there's a slide!!"

Sweetie leaped into the air, and she slid down the handle of the spoon on her behind. "WHEEEEE!"

"It's not a—!" yelled Sugar.

Sweetie landed with a thud, flipping

Doreen Cronin

the spoon right out of the hole.
"—pool," finished Sugar.
"Wow," said Sweetie.
"I thought that would

be more fun. But I'm sure it will be way better when Poppy gets here with the floaties."

"What?" asked Dirt and Sugar.

"Wheeeeeeee!" Poppy's fluffy yellow body blocked the sun as he flew into the hole and landed on top of them.

"Worst pool ever," mumbled Sweetie from the bottom of the pile.

Chapter 2

"For the last time," Sugar protested as she stood balanced atop Poppy, Dirt, and Sweetie, "this is NOT A POOL!" Sugar then pulled herself up over the edge of the nonpool.

"What is it then?" Dirt asked as Sugar then reached down for Poppy and pulled her out. Poppy held on to Sugar's legs as she reached down farther into the hole for Dirt. Then Dirt held Poppy who held Sugar who reached farther still for Sweetie.

"It's a storm shelter," answered Sugar, lowering her voice, "to keep us safe."

"Is there a big storm coming?" Poppy snuggled up close to Sweetie.

"There's always a storm coming,

kid," replied Sugar. "I've been watching those Connolly kids next door, and they've been moving all kinds of things into their garage. A little bit every day. They know something is coming, and now I know something is coming too."

"Really??" All the yellow drained from Poppy's face.

"I've already checked the weather report for today, Poppy," Dirt said reassuringly. "There are no storms in the forecast at all."

"Maybe not *today*. Maybe not *here*," announced Sugar. "But mark my words, kid, somewhere in the world, a storm is brewing at this very moment."

"Is that true???" Poppy cried out.

"Sort of," explained Dirt reluctantly, shooting Sugar a dirty look. "Storms happen when warm, moist air meets up with cool air. And, well, there's a lot of air warming and cooling around the planet, pretty much all the time. So, yes, there is probably a storm brewing *somewhere* in the world right now."

"That is exactly what I just said," Sugar remarked.

"It really isn't," replied Dirt.

"Listen, whether it strikes today or tomorrow or next week doesn't matter," said Sugar. "What matters is that we are prepared for it! There is absolutely no way to know when a storm will strike."

Poppy jumped into Sweetie's arms.

"Actually, scientists can watch storms as they develop and track them *very* closely by satellite and radar," explained Dirt, unfolding Poppy's legs one at time and coaxing him back to the ground.

"Wow! I want to be a scientist," said Sweetie. "They know all kinds of things."

"You'd make an excellent meteorologist, Sweetie," suggested Dirt.

"What's a meteorologist?" asked Sweetie.

"A person who studies meteors,

kid," said Sugar. "Pay attention!"

"Actually," said Dirt, writing the word in her notebook, "*meteo* is Greek for 'from the atmosphere' and *ologist* is a suffix that means 'someone who studies something.' So a *meteorologist* is a person who studies the weather."

"Because weather comes from the atmosphere!" said Sweetie.

"Exactly! Lots of the words we use today actually come from Greek or Latin," continued Dirt.

"Seems like an awful lot of work just to say weatherman," said Sugar. "*Weather* meaning 'weather' and *man* meaning 'man.'"

"You mean weather*person*," added Poppy.

"Actually, Dirt is on to something!" said Sugar, ignoring Poppy's remark. "Whether it strikes today or tomorrow or next week doesn't matter. What matters is that we are prepared. And this *meteor* shelter will keep us prepared. There is absolutely no way to predict when a meteor will strike."

"What's a meteor?" asked Sugar.

"A meteor is a rock from outer space," Dirt explained. "It's very rare for a meteor to crash to Earth. Most of the time it simply burns up long before it reaches the ground."

"Like I said, space rocks are hard to predict," said Sugar.

Poppy and Sweetie waited for Dirt to reply.

"Sugar might be right about that," said Dirt.

"So why don't we just stay in the shelter all the time so we'll always be safe?" said Poppy.

"That's no way to live, kid," said Sugar.

"Sugar's right," said Dirt. "You have to be out in the world, with all its risks and unpredictability, in order to live a full life."

"NO, I meant in a small hole with too many chickens. THAT is absolutely no way to live," explained Sugar.

"Now that you mention it, that hole isn't really big enough for everybody," remarked Dirt. "J. J. is definitely not going to fit in there."

"Listen, kid. You can't have a dog in a meteor shelter," said Sugar.

"Why not?" asked Poppy.

"Dogs are notorious for making people angry," Sugar answered.

"Dogs are actually notorious for providing comfort and unconditional love," said Dirt. "Why wouldn't you want one in a meteor shelter?

"Flatulence," declared Sugar.

"What does *flatulence* mean?" asked Poppy.

"It's Latin for 'who cut the cheese,'" replied Sugar.

"What about Mom?" asked Sweetie, her voice cracking. "I don't think she's

going to fit in the shelter either."

"Moms are notorious for making people angry too," answered Sugar.

"What??" asked Dirt.

"Why?" gulped Sweetie.

"Same reason," answered Sugar. "It's unbearable."

"I've never heard that," said Dirt, her hands on her hips now.

"Sometimes they're silent," explained Sugar.

"That's not what I meant!" cried Dirt, now standing directly in front of Sugar. "Who *exactly* is this shelter going to protect?"

"Right now, just us. Although, to be

honest, it's really only comfortable for three, so in case of a meteor, last one there is a rotten egg."

"Sugar, if you want to build a storm-meteor shelter, that's . . . fine . . . I guess," said Dirt. "But it really should be big enough for everybody."

"Every man, woman, and child for themselves," said Sugar. "It's in the United States Constitution."

Poppy and Sweetie waited for Dirt to reply.

"That is absolutely not in the United States Constitution," declared Dirt. "But this does seem like the kind of thing we should vote on."

"Great idea!" said Sweetie.

"That is a terrible idea, Sweetie," said Sugar. "Where in the world did you get such a terrible idea, Dirt?"

"The United States Constitution," replied Dirt.

"That is absolutely not in the Constitution," said Sugar.

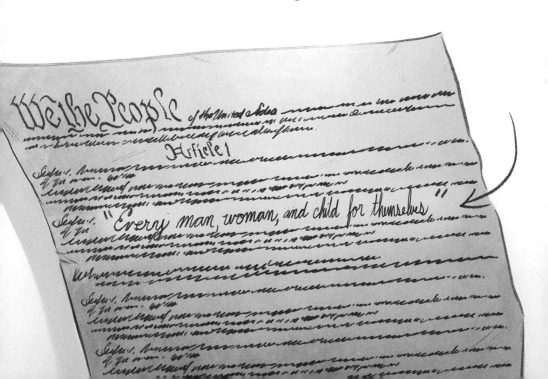

Poppy and Sweetie waited for Dirt to reply.

"It absolutely is," replied Dirt.

"Fine," sighed Sugar.

"Great," said Dirt. "We'll all take some time to think it through, we'll schedule a debate, and then we'll vote. Agreed?"

"Agreed," declared Sweetie.

"Agreed," said Poppy.

"Agreed," said Sugar.

Chapter 3

SHING!

FOOSH!

PLOP!

"A little help here!" announced Sugar from the bottom of the hole the next morning. Dirt rubbed the sleep out of her eyes and marched toward the unfinished shelter.

SHING!

FOOSH!

PLOP!

A spoonful of dirt landed at her feet.

SHING!

FOOSH!

"I thought we agreed to vote on this," Dirt protested from the edge of the hole.

PLOP!

"We did. This morning, at three thirty, in the spare tire under the blue tarp in the Connolly's garage next door," said Sugar. "I was the only one there."

"Three thirty in the morning?!" cried Dirt. "Under a tarp?"

"Voting is not always convenient," replied Sugar.

"Sugar," Dirt replied, "if we had *known* the vote was at three thirty under the tarp in the Connolly's garage, we would have voted against the shelter—and you know it."

Poppy and Sweetie arrived sleepy-eyed at the hole.

Sugar leaned her spoon against the side of the hole and walked up the handle. "Fine. Everybody's here. Let's vote now."

"Thank you, Sugar," said Dirt. "All in favor of a shelter for everybody—"

"Not so fast, kid," interrupted

Sugar. "What's the password?"

"Password?" asked Dirt.

"The secret password you need to vote," explained Sugar.

"A secret password to vote? That's unconstitutional!"

Dirt and Sugar stared at each other from opposite sides of the hole.

"Sorry, kid. Time's up," Sugar said finally. "The correct answer was SHELEILA."

"Sugggarrrrrr!" growled Dirt.

"Seems to me that if you've got some special voting rules—like 'no passwords'—you should have mentioned it yesterday," said Sugar. "It's important for voting rules to be very clear. Don't you agree?"

"Fine," said Dirt. "Next time no passwords, and we all need to know in advance WHEN the vote is going to take place and WHERE the vote is going to take place."

"Deal." Sugar jerked her head toward

the hole. Poppy and Sweetie jumped in.

"Oooh!" oozed Sweetie. "Where did you get all these shiny spoons?"

"Over there," replied Sugar, without pointing her wing in any particular direction.

"Over where?" asked Dirt.

"Garage sale," replied Sugar.

"Huh?" asked Dirt.

"Garbage," replied Sugar.

"What?!" cried Dirt.

"Squirrels," replied Sugar.

SHING! SHING!

FOOSH! FOOSH!

Two spoonfuls of dirt flew out of the hole.

PLOP!

PLOP!

Sugar motioned for Dirt to get to work.

Dirt refused to move.

"Suit yourself," replied Sugar, "but when a giant space rock is hurtling toward Earth at the speed of light with an impact not seen since the extinction of the dinosaurs and the cavemen, you're going to wish you were in here!"

"Wait a minute," said Poppy from the hole. "How is a hole going to keep us safe from a giant space rock hurtling toward Earth at the speed of light?"

"I haven't worked out all the details yet, kid," said Sugar. "We might need some kind of door."

"I don't understand you, Sugar," said Dirt.

"That's because you are not a Sugarologist!" yelled Sweetie from the hole.

SHING!

FOOSH!

PLOP!

"That's not a word, Sweetie," remarked Dirt, avoiding another *plop* launching out of the hole.

"And you, madam, are clearly not a wordologist," Sugar remarked.

SHING!

FOOSH!

PLOP!

"I CAN'T BE a wordologist!! It's not a real thing!!" Dirt was exasperated.

"Mom says you can be anything you want to be, Dirt," said Poppy from the hole. "Don't you ever forget it!"

SHING!

CLUNK!

"What was that?" asked Dirt.

"I'm not sure," answered Sweetie from the hole. "Does anybody know a good clunkologist?"

Dirt let out a heavy sigh.

"Probably just a rock," said Sugar.

SHING!

CLUNK!

"Doesn't look like a rock," announced Sweetie.

Dirt left Sugar standing at the edge

of the hole and jumped in, where something long, hard, and smooth lay partially uncovered at the bottom. Dirt brushed off the area around it to get a closer look. After a few moments of concentration, Dirt finally spoke.

"This is not a rock," said Dirt in her most serious voice.

"What is it?" asked Sugar.

"Poppy, Sweetie," said Dirt, "I think you may have uncovered a bone."

Chapter 4

"What kind of b-b-b-bone?" asked Poppy, taking a giant backward step away from their discovery.

"Dinosaur," announced Sugar. "Female. *T. rex.* leg bone."

"I think we need more infor—" said Dirt.

"Let's vote on it," interrupted Sugar.

"Here and now with no passwords. Who says it's the leg bone of female *T. rex?*"

"I do," said Sweetie.

"I do," said Poppy.

"I do," said Sugar. "And there you have it."

"That's not the kind of thing you vote on, Sugar," said Dirt.

"Who thinks Dirt is unconstitutional?" asked Sugar, raising her wing.

"I do," said Sweetie.

"I do," said Poppy.

"I do," said Sugar.

Dirt sat on her bottom, crossed her legs, closed her eyes, and took a long, deep breath. *"If* it *is* a bone, then we need to treat it very, very carefully."

"Dirt's right," said Sugar. "That *T. rex* bone has probably been here since the meteor struck a hundred years ago, wiping out the dinosaurs and all the cavemen."

"Cave *people,* Sugar," Sweetie corrected her. "Cave *people."*

"Um, Sugar, a moment?" Dirt pulled her sister to the side. "Before you get Poppy and Sweetie too excited, I think a timeline might be helpful here." Dirt opened her notebook and drew a timeline showing the millions of years between the dinosaur extinction and the existence of cave people.

"I think you're forgetting something, Dirt," said Sugar.

"What's that?"

"Unicorns," said Sugar.

"Unicorns aren't extinct," Dirt explained. "They never existed."

"Then how do we know what they looked like?" asked Sugar.

Dinosaurs Evolve ↓ 228

Dinosaurs Extinct ↓ 65

people ↓ now

300

Millions of Years Ago

"Well . . . because . . . ," Dirt began. "Um, that's not really a fair question. . . ."

"Sounds like something we should vote on," said Sugar.

"You can't *vote* unicorns into existence!" declared Dirt.

"As I was saying," Sugar announced, ignoring Dirt's protest and turning back to Poppy and Sweetie. "The shelter is now also an important scientific-discovery site, and the spoons are no longer the proper tools for excavation."

"That much I agree with," said Dirt.

"So," continued Sugar, "we're going to need the power tools and the blowtorch from the Connolly's garage—"

"Sugar," said Dirt, "for starters, we do not have permission to go into the Connolly's garage."

"If I remember, avoiding the Connolly's garage is what cost you the vote last time," said Sugar. "You might want to reconsider."

"Sugar, we need to treat the bone *carefully*," said Dirt.

"Dirt has a point," agreed Sugar. "Grab all the brushes you can find in the house—paintbrushes, tooth-brushes, hairbrushes," said Sugar. "But NOT the round yellow brush in the bathroom!"

"Will it damage the bone?" asked Poppy.

"No, I use that one for volume after I shampoo," replied Sugar.

"I've always wondered how you got your feathers so fluffy," Poppy exclaimed.

"I find a little hair spray at the roots really helps too," Sugar said with a wink.

"I love Sugarology!" said Poppy.

"How do we get into the house?" asked Sweetie.

"Just move the pot of chrysanthemums next to the hose," explained Sugar.

"Why?" asked Poppy.

"Because then you can remove the loose brick that doesn't look like a loose brick, because I put it back so carefully after I removed it," Sugar replied.

"Ooh, how did you do that?" asked Poppy.

"With some power tools and a blow-torch I borrowed from the Connolly's garage—"

"What?!" cried Dirt.

"Sugarology is fun!" said Sweetie as she and Poppy ran toward the chrysanthemums. "I'm learning so much!"

Chapter 5

A few minutes later, Sweetie arrived back at the hole with a canful of paintbrushes.

"Where's Poppy?" asked Sugar.

"I'm not sure," answered Sweetie, alarmed. "I thought he was right behind me!"

A minute later, Poppy strolled out of

the house with a handful of brushes. Sweetie gasped. Poppy's head was the size of a cantaloupe.

"Poppy, your feathers are very, very . . . big," said Sweetie.

"I think you mean *voluminous*," he answered.

"That too," said Sugar. "You didn't happen to use the yellow hairbrush while you were in there?"

"Nope," Poppy answered.

"I see," said Sugar, maintaining steady eye contact.

"I used the green one," Poppy admitted.

"Interesting choice," said Sugar.

An acorn ricocheted off Poppy's face. He didn't flinch.

"And the hair spray?" asked Sugar.

"A little," Poppy admitted.

"Just the roots, kid," whispered Sugar. "Just the roots."

"Too much?" asked Poppy, embarrassed.

"Rookie mistake," said
Sugar. "We'll try to scrape
it off later. But in the meantime, you're
highly flammable, so stay away from
the blowtorch."

"Ahem," Dirt interrupted. "Before
we get back to the bone, I'd like to
show you something I showed Sugar
while you were in the house. I think

it will help you understand what's in the hole and what it might—or might not—be." Dirt held up her timeline.

Poppy and Sweetie studied it for a moment.

"I think you're forgetting something, Dirt," said Sweetie.

"What's that?" asked Dirt, tapping her pencil.

"Unicorns," answered Poppy.

"Dirt says unicorns never existed," said Sugar with an eye roll.

"Then how do we know what they looked like?" asked Poppy.

Poppy and Sweetie waited for Dirt to reply.

Dirt had no reply.

"So it *could* be a unicorn bone?" asked Sweetie.

"Absolutely not," said Dirt.

"Who thinks it could be a unicorn bone?" asked Sugar.

"I do," said Poppy, raising his wing.

"I do," said Sweetie, raising her wing.

"I do," said Sugar, raising her wing.

"You can't vote unicorns into existence!!" declared Dirt for the second time.

"Okay, kid," said Sugar. "But you can't complain about the outcome if you don't vote."

Poppy and Sweetie waited for Dirt to reply.

"Fine." Dirt let out a heavy sigh. "I vote that it is not a unicorn bone."

"Sorry, kid," said Sugar, counting wings in the air. "You lost again. You're not very good at this voting thing, are you?"

"Or at Sugarology," added Sweetie.

"That's enough Dirtology for today," said Sugar. "Everybody, back in the hole!"

"Wait," said Dirt. "We have to organize this the right way so we can keep track of our discoveries." Dirt held out a box of wooden stakes. "We'll place these in the ground to create a rectangle at the bottom of the hole. Then we'll run string from one stake to another to create a grid, labeling it *1, 2, 3, 4, 5* and *A, B, C, D, E.*

"We found the bone, here, at C2, extending into D3," Dirt continued. "So that's how we record it on the grid."

Sugar, Poppy, and Sweetie nodded in agreement.

"If you find something new, we'll enter that on the grid too," Dirt continued.

Sugar, Poppy, and Sweetie nodded in agreement again.

"Sugar, you'll take D5. Sweetie, you'll take D4. And Poppy, why don't you take C1?"

"BINGO!" yelled Sugar.

Dirt glared at her sister.

"Just a little *T. rex*-grid humor, kid," said Sugar.

Poppy and Sweetie waited for Dirt to laugh.

Dirt did not laugh.

"To the shelter!" cried Sugar. Poppy, Sweetie, and Dirt returned to the bone as Sugar set up stakes and roped off the area around the perimeter of the hole. Then she hung a sign: RESTRICTED AREA, before jumping into the dig with the rest of the squad.

SWISH!

Sugar used a toothbrush to gently clear an area in D5.

SWISH!

Sweetie used a paintbrush to gently clear away an area in D4.

SWISH.

Dirt used her own wing to gently brush an area in A2.

SWISH.

Poppy used a vegetable brush to gently clear an area in C1.

"What are you kids doing down there?" asked Moosh, appearing at the edge of the hole.

"Digging up a female *T. rex* leg bone from one hundred years ago," said Sugar, not looking up.

"Where did you get all those brushes?" asked Moosh, stepping even closer to the hole, momentarily losing her balance as she tipped too close to the edge. She steadied herself and then repeated the question. "The brushes?"

Poppy and Sweetie waited for Dirt to reply.

Dirt had no reply.

BOINK!

BOINK!

Two acorns landed at Moosh's feet, and she immediately spun around and spotted a group of squirrels across the yard. "Hey!" yelled Sugar. "You can't throw acorns at my mom!"

Moosh took slow, deliberate steps toward the squirrels as they huddled closer and closer together, each pointing a finger at the squirrel next to them. Sugar followed at her side. "I'll take it from here, Sugar," said Moosh.

"You go dig up that female *T. rex* leg bone while I have a little chat about backyard etiquette with our friends here."

"Close call!" said Sugar, leaping back into the hole. "We almost got busted with the brushes!"

"I can't believe they threw acorns at Mom," said Sweetie. "I mean that is just . . . unconstitutional!"

"The Constitution doesn't actually cover throwing things at someone's mom," said Dirt.

"It should!" declared Poppy.

"I threw the acorns, kid," Sugar admitted.

"What??" Dirt shrieked.

"You threw acorns at your own mother????" gasped Poppy. "*That* is definitely unconstitutional, right, Dirt???"

"I'm afraid not," said Dirt.

"I did what had to be done, kid. You want to uncover a one-hundred-year-old female *T. rex* leg bone, or do you want be grounded for the rest of the month?"

"But you were in the hole with us! How did you do that?" asked Sweetie.

"When I originally planned the shelter, I dug an emergency tunnel that runs from here to the coop. I just ducked out for a second while Mom was focusing on her balance. I scurried

behind the squirrels, lobbed the acorns, and then predicted that they would turn on one another when they realized Mom was headed their way."

"Advanced Sugarology," said Sweetie. "It's so hard to keep up!!"

Dirt let out a heavy sigh.

The squad went back to work.

SWISH.

SWISH.

SWISH.

SWISH.

"I found something!" Poppy screeched. "I found something!"

"What is it?" asked Sweetie.

"I'm not sure," said Poppy, "but it's round!"

"OOH!" said Sweetie, leaning in closer.

"It's blue!" marveled Poppy.

"OOH!" said Sweetie, leaning in closer still.

"And it's so pretty!" said Poppy.

"That's an eyeball!" shrieked Sweetie, taking a giant step away from their discovery.

"Let's mark it on the grid," said Dirt, jotting the new find down in her notebook grid.

"Do you see what I see?" asked Sweetie.

"I'm not sure," said Poppy, still considering the diagram. "What do you see?"

"The bone is not a female *T. rex* leg bone, it's a horn!" She borrowed Dirt's pencil.

"OH MY GOSH!" declared Poppy. "It's a prehistoric blue-eyed unicorn!"

"What we have here," said Sugar, "is now the world's first meteor-storm-prehistoric-unicorn–preserving shelter. It's unprecedented."

SHING!!

FLOOSH!

A spoonful of dirt rained down into the hole.

PLOP!

Quickly followed by two more.

PLOP!

PLOP!

Sugar stuck her head up out of the hole. The squirrels were digging a hole of their own in the shade of the oak tree.

"What are you doing?" demanded

Sugar as she scrambled out of the hole and ran across the yard. Gray Squirrel held up her hand and pointed to the sign: RESTRICTED AREA—SQUIRRELS ONLY.

"What does it look like we're doing?" asked Gray Squirrel from the other side of the rope.

"It looks like you're digging," Sugar said calmly. "But you can't dig here, buddy. We've unearthed a rare scientific find. It's a prehistoric

unicorn. And we don't know what area we may need to dig up next. Got me?"

"Unicorns don't exist, chicken. But nice try," answered the squirrel. "We know you're digging a chickens-only shelter. So we're digging one for the squirrels."

"Wrong again, squirrel," said Sugar. "We *were* digging a chickens-only shelter, but now it's a meteor-storm-prehistoric-unicorn–preserving shelter."

SHING!

FLOOSH!

PLOP.

"Where did you get those spoons?" asked Sugar, eyeballing the collection in the squirrel hole.

"Over there," said the squirrel, pointing in no particular direction.

"Over where?" demanded Sugar.

"Garage sale," said a squirrel, knee-deep in the hole.

"Huh?" said Sugar.

"Garbage," said another squirrel, knee-deep in the hole.

"What?" asked Sugar.

"Santa," said another squirrel, knee-deep in the hole.

Sugar leaned in for a closer look and gasped. "Everybody knows you don't dig holes with a teaspoon!" she yelled. "HAVE YOU NO CIVILITY??"

The squirrels ignored Sugar's outburst and the digging continued.

SHOOSH!

FOOSH!

PLOP! PLOP! PLOP! PLOP!

"What is the hole for?" asked Dirt when she arrived. Poppy and Sweetie were right behind her.

"Protection," answered Gray Squirrel

from the other side of the rope.

"From a meteor?" guessed Dirt. "Meteor strikes are pretty rare, you know."

"Nope," replied the squirrel.

"Hurricane?" guessed Sweetie.

"Meteorologists are actually very good at tracking them."

"Nope," replied the squirrel.

"Then what? What are *you* afraid of?" asked Poppy.

"Your mom," answered the squirrels in the hole. "She's really scary when she's mad."

Poppy and Sweetie waited for Dirt to respond.

But Sugar broke the silence.

"You're going to need some kind of door," said Sugar.

"Big one," added Dirt.

Chapter 6

Back at their own hole, the chickens were now deep in discussion.

"I vote that we order them to stop their dig," announced Sugar. "We don't know what else is buried under here, and we can't risk anybody else damaging things we haven't found yet! What if there is an entire

Doreen Cronin

unicorn village under our feet??"

"We can't stop their dig," said Dirt. "It's their yard too."

"But they restricted an area—you

can't just go ahead and restrict an area. Chickens need to roam!"

"We restricted this area," Dirt pointed out.

"That's different! We found a pre-historic unicorn village!!" said Sweetie.

"We actually don't know what we've found . . . yet," said Dirt.

"You know what?? Let them dig," said Sugar. "They're using teaspoons! At that rate, they'll still be knee-deep come Christmas. Back to the hole!"

SWISH.

SWISH.

SWISH.

SWISH.

"I found something!" Sweetie
screeched. "I found something!"

"What is it?" asked Dirt.

"It's long," said Sweetie. The squad
moved in closer.

"OOOH, and it's sharp!" marveled
Sweetie. The squad moved in closer.

"And it's so shiny!" added Sweetie.

"That's a claw!" shrieked Poppy.

"That's impossible!" remarked Sweetie.

"Why?" asked Poppy.

"Because unicorns don't have claws!" said Sweetie.

"Let's put it on the grid," said Dirt.

"Interesting," remarked Dirt.

"I found something too!" said Sugar.

"What is it?" the squad said at the same time.

"It's round and it's green," announced Sugar.

"It's . . . another eye!" announced Sweetie.

Dirt plotted it on the grid.

"I don't think that's a unicorn," said Poppy.

"What is it?" asked Sweetie.

"Allow me," said Sugar, taking the pencil from above Dirt's ear.

"It's a *T. rex*!" declared Poppy. "With a unicorn's eyeball in its stomach!"

"The dinosaurs *ate* all the uni-corns??" asked Sweetie, all the yellow draining from her face.

"Mystery solved, kid," announced Sugar, looking a bit queasy herself.

Poppy and Sweetie waited for Dirt to respond.

"I don't think we have the whole picture yet," Dirt said.

"We have plenty!" said Sugar. "I mean, just look at the grid! It couldn't be more clear!"

"Well, it is a little small for a *T. rex*," said Sweetie.

"We've discovered a miniature *T. rex*!" announced Sugar. "It's like the

miniature poodle of dinosaurs!"

"Or it's not a *T. rex* or a unicorn," said Poppy, borrowing the pencil from Sugar.

"It's a new kind of creature that no one has even seen before!"

"Could be," said Dirt.

"Really??" said Sugar, Poppy, and Sweetie.

"Let's put it on the list of possibilities and keep working."

T. rex
Unicorn
Miniature T. rex who ate a unicorn
Unknown mono-clawed creature with multiple eyes

SHING!
FOOSH!
A shower of dirt rained down into the hole.
PLIP.
PLIP.
PLIP.

Chapter 7

A crew of chipmunks was now digging in the corner by the vegetable garden. They had hung their own sign too: RESTRICTED AREA—CHIPMUNKS ONLY.

SHOOSH!

FOOSH!

PLIP!

"What do you guys think you're doing?" Sugar demanded.

"Digging a shelter. Chipmunks only," replied the chipmunk in charge.

"Why?" asked Dirt. "What are you afraid of?"

"We don't know. But you're digging, and the squirrels are digging, so clearly there's something to be afraid of, so we are digging our own, just in case."

"Just in case . . . what?" asked Dirt.

"Just in case the thing that we don't know about happens," said the chipmunk, suddenly trembling. A low grumble began to fill the air around them. "And I think it's happening right now!!"

"What is that sound?" asked Sugar. "Are you flatulating?!!"

"That's not a word, Sug—" said Dirt.

The low grumble grew to a deafening ROOOOAAAARRRRRR!! The chipmunks tried to jump into their shelter, but the wind blew the pile of dirt right back into the hole, filling it up.

"FOLLOW ME!!!" yelled Sugar, heading for the emergency tunnel

inside the chickens' shelter. Dirt and the chipmunks fell in line behind Sugar while large white balls of hail began to pelt them.

"IT'S A TORNADO!!" shrieked the squirrels. They jumped into their shelter, but it wasn't deep enough to protect them. They tried scurrying up the tree for safety, until the branches bent in the wind but dropping the squirrels back to the ground.

"Now it's a hurricane!" yelled Poppy and Sweetie as buckets and Frisbees

and lawn chairs spun past them.

"GET DOWN! GET DOWN!" shouted Sugar. The chipmunks and the squirrels and the chickens got as low as they could, flattening themselves.

"THIS WAY!" A furry face was sticking out of the entrance to Sugar's emergency tunnel. The frightened animals dove in and traveled through the now-widened tunnel, just as something dark came hurtling toward the door, completely blocking out the sun.

Chapter 8

BOINK!

   BOINK!

     SPLAT!

      CLUNK!

Plastic furniture, wood scraps, toys, and even a Big Wheel clattered across the yard, slamming into the chicken coop. All the animals huddled together for safety. Then the chicken coop itself was wrapped in darkness.

"Is it a tornado?" asked one of the chipmunks.

"It *can* get very dark before and during a tornado," said Sweetie. "But I'm not seeing the telltale cylinder."

"I think it's a hurricane!" said one of

the squirrels. "The wind is so strong!"

"A hurricane *can* have winds up to two hundred miles per hour," said Sweetie, "but torrential rain is more typical."

"It must be a meteor!" said Poppy, his face feathers still perfectly in place. "I saw something big and dark coming toward the door!"

"Unlikely," said Sweetie. "We would have felt the impact. But . . . it could be a *derecho*."

They all stared at her.

"It's a wind shear accompanying a strong line or wall of thunderstorms. Some say it comes from the Spanish word for *straight*," Sweetie explained.

They all stared at her.

"A girl can study Sugarology, astronomy, and meteorology at the same time, you know!" answered Sweetie.

Suddenly, just as quickly as it had begun, the roaring and the wind stopped.

Dirt and Sugar told everyone to stay put and slowly opened the door to the chicken coop, pulling aside a familiar dark-blue tarp that had blown onto the chicken coop door.

"It wasn't a tornado, a hurricane, a hailstorm, a meteor, or a *derecho*!" announced Sugar.

"What was it???" asked Sweetie.

"It was the Connolly kids with a leaf

blower and a crate full of Ping-Pong balls," Dirt explained.

"I'm not gonna lie," said Sugar. "That wasn't on my list."

"I have a question," said Poppy.

"Yes?" asked Sugar.

"Who is that?" Sticking out of the entrance to the emergency tunnel was that same adorable fuzzy face that had led them through the tunnel.

"I believe that is a *bog lemming*," said Dirt.

"Wow. I didn't think they actually existed," said Poppy.

"Bog lemmings are small rodents who dig underground burrows," said

Dirt. "My guess is that all the digging in the yard might have been interfering with her home."

"If I'm not mistaken," said Sugar, "she's the one who widened the tunnel so it would be big enough for all of us to make it to the coop."

The bog lemming winked and disappeared back into the tunnel without another word.

Epilogue

The Connolly kids took off in a flash when they saw Moosh sprinting in their direction. She cleared that fence by an easy foot, and the back door to the Connolly's house wasn't strong enough to keep her out. The Connolly kids found themselves between a rock and a hard place: the rock being

Moosh and the hard place being, well, Mrs. Connolly. I don't think they'll be allowed outside for the rest of the summer. I picked Moosh up by the scruff of her neck and carried her back out the giant Moosh-shaped hole in the door.

Everything that had been buried

in the yard came to light, including the *T. rex*–eating unicorn, which was in reality a gardening tool and some marbles. Nope, wasn't on my list, either.

The squad and the chipmunks and the squirrels all worked together to make something out of the scrap wood, the Ping-Pong balls, the marbles, the gardening tool, and everything

else they gathered up from the yard.

"I think we should call it *E Pluribus Unum*," announced Dirt.

"It's Latin for 'one big hole,'" said Sugar, tearing up with emotion.

"No, it's Latin for 'out of many, one,'" explained Dirt. "It means that when all of us come together, we make one. Whether we are chickens, chipmunks, dogs, squirrels, or butterflies. And we are stronger that way."

"That works too," Sugar admitted.

The statue stands at the entrance to the pool they had all dug together. Dirt is a no-nonsense lifeguard; Sweetie keeps an eye on the weather;

and Poppy's giant head appears to be waterproof, too.

"I'm not gonna lie," said Sugar. "I think those Connolly kids could really use a little more adult supervision. They cause all kinds of trouble out here."

That's when I pushed her into the pool.